My Abuelita

WRITTEN BY **Tony Johnston**

ILLUSTRATED BY **Yuyi Morales**

PHOTOGRAPHED BY **Tim O'Meara**

HARCOURT CHILDREN'S BOOKS
HOUGHTON MIFFLIN HARCOURT
Boston   New York   2009

The illustrations in this book were created with polymer clay, wire,
felting wool, acrylic paints, fabric, wood, metals, and Mexican crafts,
then photographed and digitally manipulated.

The text type was set in Black Bead and PuiTaiChi.
The display type was set in LD Bohemian Filigree.

Library of Congress Cataloging-in-Publication
Control Number 2006006872
ISBN 978-0-15-216330-3

Printed in Singapore

TWP 10 9 8 7 6 5 4 3 2 1

For storytellers
everywhere
—T.J.

For the abuelas:
the grandmothers of all shapes
and colors (even the regañonas)
who open their arms to love a
child with all their corazón
—Y.M.

abuelita

yo

I live with my grandma. And she lives with me. I call her Abuelita. She is as old as the hills, she says. Maybe older. Her hair is the color of salt. Her face is as crinkled as a dried chile.

But that doesn't matter. She is my abuelita. I love her. And she loves me. My abuelita also loves her work.

Each day she wakes up with the sun.
She stretches this way and that with her
cat—named Frida Kahlo—and with me,
limbering up for work.

She does knee bends and breathes deep,
oh, deep. Like a big salty whale out at
sea. I do the same. Frida Kahlo is already
limber, so she tilts her head this way and
that, watching Abuelita and me.

My abuelita is round. Robust, she says, like a calabaza. A pumpkin. She doesn't mind. She likes pumpkins.

"Being round gives me a good round voice," she tells me. "Just the voice for my work."

After she stretches, my abuelita takes a shower. While the water splashes, she sings way down in her throat. Deep, boggy, froggy notes that stretch her voice, for work.

"¡Ay! Isn't it thrilling to sing like a frog?" she asks me.

I sing deep and boggy, froggy notes:

"GLUB! GLUB! GLUB!"

"It is very thrilling," I agree.

Then my abuelita wraps herself in a towel striped with black and yellow. She looks like a great big bee. While she dries, she hums like a great big bee, getting ready for work. I hum, too, for fun.

Abuelita puts on her fuzzy robe and prepares breakfast—
fresh orange juice, *queso*, cheese, warm tortillas she has
made by hand, and *huevos estrellados*, starry eggs. That is,
fried. While she cooks, she yodels about bedroom slippers.
"¡Pantuflas—pantuflas—pantuflas!"

"Yodeling loosens my voice," she explains, "for work."

I know that already. My abuelita says it every day. But
I like to hear it anyway.

Frida Kahlo likes the *pantuflas* song,
so she sings, too. She sings so nicely, Abuelita
gives her a taste of starry eggs. Then I yodel,
"¡Pantuflas—pantuflas—pantuflas!"
I yodel so nicely, my abuelita gives me
eggs. I give some to Frida Kahlo. We
yodel and yodel. Oodles of yodels.
Frida gets oodles of starry eggs.

Abuelita is almost ready for work.
"Just one last thing," she tells me.
"What?" I ask, even though I already know.
"Now," she whispers, "comes my booming."
I plug my ears just in time.
Then my abuelita booms out words, loud
and clear. She always says the words should
be as round as dimes and as wild as blossoms
blooming.

Soon she stops.

"¡Ay! I feel like a wild blossom blooming," my abuelita says. "I must be ready for work."

"You're not ready," I say.

"What's missing?" she asks, looking at herself carefully.

Fold tabs

Fold tabs

"Your clothes." I laugh. She's still in her fuzzy robe.

"¡Ay—ay—ay! I almost forgot!" My abuelita always says that.

She puts on a flowery gown and bright
red shoes and a scarf like a cloud that flows
down to the ground.
"Am I ready?"
"You're not ready."

"What is missing?" my abuelita asks Frida Kahlo. Frida Kahlo meows because she doesn't know. She just knows that she likes eggs that look like stars.

"Your things!" I say.

Abuelita's hands fly to her face. "¡Ay! What would I do without you?" She always says that, too.

We stuff her carcacha, her jalopy, with all the things she needs for work: a temple with many skinny stairs; rustling stalks of maize; a magnificent plumed snake; a king and queen as brown as beans; a calaca, skeleton; one sun; one moon; one feathered crown.

"Am I ready now?"

"¡Sí!"

"Then, vámonos! Let's go! ¡Besitos!" My abuelita blows kisses to Frida Kahlo. So do I. While she curls up in the sun, we drive to work. As we roll along, Abuelita's cloud-scarf billows behind.

¡Bienvenidos!
Welcome!

At last we arrive at a big brick building. My abuelita
swoops in. So do I. We love to swoop.

Abuelita arranges her things. I help. She arranges herself.
I help. Last of all, I crown her with a sweep of stars.

"Am I ready?" my abuelita asks me.

"You're ready."

An audience crowds close. Like
many worms, it squirms around—because
it's an audience of girls and boys. My abuelita
raises a hand and everyone sort of settles down.
Then, with words as wild as blossoms
blooming, as round as dimes, she begins.
"Once upon a time . . ."

When I am old and pumpkin-shaped and my hair is the color of salt and my face is crinkled like a dried chile, I know that is what I want to be—

a storyteller like my abuelita.